A CHRISTMAS LIKE HELEN'S

Natalie Kinsey–Warnock ✿ *Illustrated by Mary Azarian*

HOUGHTON MIFFLIN COMPANY

BOSTON 2004

In loving memory of my grandmother, Helen Urie Rowell — N.K.-W.

*In fondest memory of my grandfather, William Harvey Hatch,
and my mother, Eleanor Hatch Schneider, whose Christmases were like Helen's. — M.A.*

GLOSSARY OF TERMS

Scrogglings—a Scottish word for small, runty apples
left on the trees after the harvest

Pung—a boxlike sleigh

Text copyright © 2004 by Natalie Kinsey-Warnock
Illustrations copyright © 2004 by Mary Azarian

www.houghtonmifflinbooks.com

The text of this book is set in 16.5-point ITC Golden Cockerel.
The illustrations are woodcuts, hand-tinted with watercolors.
Typography by Carol Goldenberg

ISBN-13   978-0-618-23137-9   ISBN-10   0-618-23137-4

Library of Congress Cataloging-in-Publication Data

Kinsey-Warnock, Natalie.
A Christmas like Helen's / by Natalie Kinsey-Warnock ; illustrated by Mary Azarian.
p. cm.
Summary: Presents a descriptive list of all the things required to have a
Christmas like the author's grandmother had, including farm animals, stories of Scotland,
ice skating in the moonlight, and joining friends, family, and neighbors at church on Christmas Eve.
ISBN 0-618-23137-4
[1. Christmas—Fiction. 2. Farm life—Vermont—Fiction. 3. Vermont—History—20th century—Fiction.] I. Azarian, Mary, ill. II. Title.
PZ7.K6293Ch 2004
[E]—dc22   2003022883

Manufactured in the United States of America
BVG 10 9 8 7 6 5 4 3 2 1

To have a Christmas like Helen's
you'll need to be born on a Vermont hill farm,
before cars, or telephones, or electricity,
and be the youngest of seven children.

You'll have to have four clever brothers
who make snow rollers and bobsleds,
who sometimes hitch themselves to a sled
and let you drive them like horses.

You must have real horses,
workhorses for sugaring and logging, plowing and mowing,
and driving horses, to pull the sleigh in winter
and the buggy in summer,
for trips to town, and to friends, and six miles to church each Sunday.

Those miles will fly by if your father
can tell stories the way Helen's father did,
of your grandfather's six-week journey from Scotland,
and of your other grandfather,
who went off to fight in the Civil War and came home a changed man,
but at least he came home.

Your mother will have stories of Scotland, too,
since she was born there. In the evenings
she'll tell of castles, and ruins, and princes in hiding,
of wailing bagpipes and stone cottages by the sea.

To have a Christmas like Helen's,
you must have a barn.
It doesn't have to be big—
a small barn will do nicely—
enough for a few Jerseys and Guernseys,
and an Ayrshire or two.
And I suppose the barn
doesn't *have* to be built by your grandfather,
hewn from trees cut on your farm,
but that would be best, of course.
The mow must be full of hay,
enough to feed the cows and horses
all winter,
and the barn cats will hide their kittens there.

You'll have to like animals:
deer that come to eat the scrogglings
from the orchard,
bears in the wild raspberry patch,
coyotes that howl at the moon,

and the farm animals:
cows, lambs, chickens, and pigs,
and cats,
especially a big black-and-white tom
that lets you dress him up
and push him around in a doll carriage.

You'll hold your sister's hand
going to the one-room schoolhouse
that's a mile from home,
and you'll walk there even on days

when it's forty degrees below zero.
You'll have to not mind
living in a place
where winter lasts nearly eight months.

You won't be thinking of Christmas
when spring finally rolls around
and the sap rises in the trees,
but the syrup you'll have
on your Christmas breakfast
must be made now.
The potatoes and corn for your Christmas feast
must be weeded all summer,
and the apples for your Christmas pies
must be picked in the fall.

You see, to have a Christmas like Helen's,
you'll need to work that land
all year long,
and know that hill farm in all its seasons.

To have a Christmas like Helen's,
your family will keep the spirit of Christmas all year long.
Your father and brothers will hay fields and cut wood
for an injured neighbor,

and when another neighbor's barn burns,
you'll help him build a new barn,
knowing that when your family needs help
your neighbors will do the same for you.

When winter blankets the hills in white,
you'll harvest ice from the pond in the woods
and snowshoe up and over every hill
to find the perfect balsam fir
and help drag it home.

To have a Christmas like Helen's,
aunts and uncles must visit,
and dozens of cousins.
You'll make snow angels in the yard
and play fox and geese.
After supper,
someone will suggest skating in the moonlight,
and even though it's late,
and cold,
and you're the youngest,
your mother lets you go,
because it's Christmas.

Everyone will have skates,
except for you,
but you'll slide on your boots
and hold hands with your cousins
to play crack-the-whip.

To have a Christmas like Helen's,
you'll have to have one Christmas
when you're sick with scarlet fever.
No one will be allowed in your room for weeks,
except your mother,
and you'll lie alone,
too sick to eat, or read,
and you won't know till days later
that the doctor didn't expect you to live.
Your parents will give you a locket
with their pictures inside,
and your father will carry you out
to see the candles on the tree,
thinking it will be your last Christmas.
But it won't.

To have a Christmas like Helen's,
you'll go to church on Christmas Eve in a hay-filled pung,
under buffalo robes and wool blankets.
The church will glow
with a candle in every window.

The minister will read the Christmas story
of Mary and Joseph and the baby born in a stable,
and you'll wonder,
Why couldn't they find room at the inn?

Then you'll bundle back into coats and boots and mittens and scarves,
with everyone calling "Merry Christmas!"
to everyone else.
You'll pile back into the pung
for the long ride home.
It will be colder now, and you'll snuggle closer to your sister.
The horses' breath will rise like plumes of smoke,
the harness bells will be ringing,
and someone will start singing
"O Holy Night,"
while overhead
the cold stars will be thick enough
to scoop up with a spoon.

You'll tumble into bed,
but later, in the middle of the night,
your father will carry you out to the barn
to see a foal being born.
You'll snuggle in the crook of his arm,
the cats curling 'round your legs,
and think,
Maybe it's not such a bad place to be born
after all.

Tomorrow,
there will be peppermint sticks and popcorn balls,
toy trucks and sleds for your brothers, and dolls for your sisters,
and the last box under the tree
will be a pair of skates just for you.

But tonight,
before the stockings and gifts under the tree,
when you're still in that barn,

tucked in the crook of your father's arm,
you know that everything you ever wanted,
or ever will want,
is right there on that farm.

*W*hen Helen grew up she had eight children and thirty-two grandchildren,
and one of those grandchildren was me.
Our Christmases aren't exactly like Helen's,
but we spend them together as family:
mother and father, sister and brothers,
aunts and uncles,
and dozens of cousins.

Helen lived her whole long life
in the place she loved best,
and I will, too.